Sssshhhh!
Brum's
off to the Big Town...

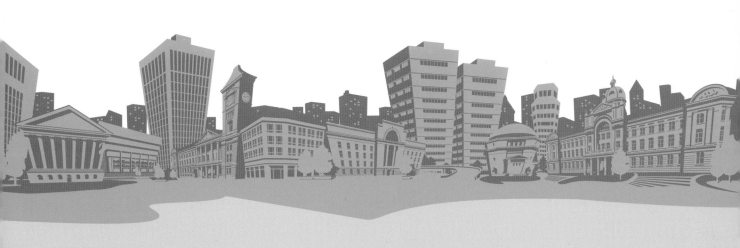

BRUM AND THE BIG TOWN BALLOONS
by Alan Dapré

British Library Cataloguing in Publication Data
A catalogue record of this book is available from the British Library.
ISBN 0 340 86597 0

First edition published 2002
10 9 8 7 6 5 4 3 2 1

Published by Hodder Children's Books
a division of Hodder Headline Limited
338 Euston Road, London, NW1 3BH

Printed in Hong Kong

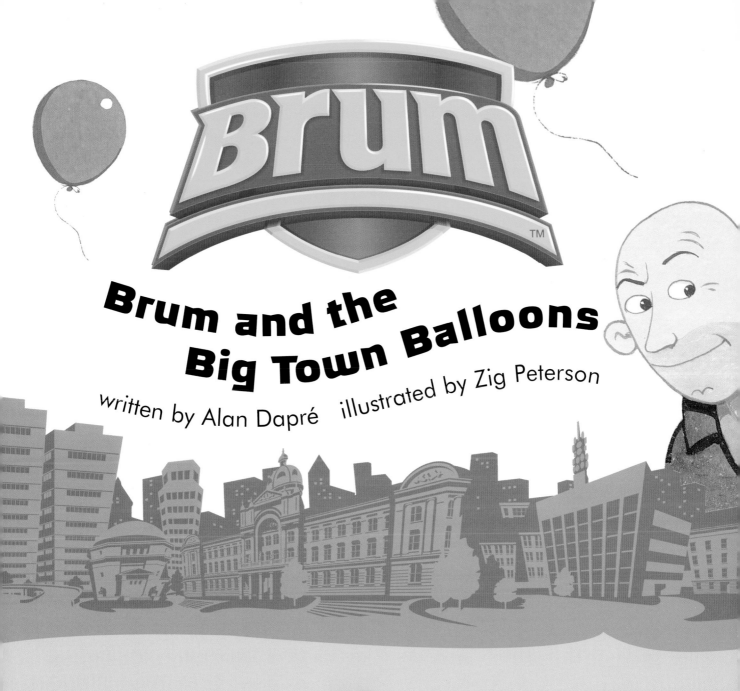

Brum

Brum and the Big Town Balloons

written by Alan Dapré   illustrated by Zig Peterson

Hodder
Children's
Books

A division of Hodder Headline Limited

It was time for a new adventure. BRUM BRUM!

The Mayor stood on the Town Hall steps. He gave Brum a big wave and proudly jiggled his shiny new balloons.

Wow - four balloons!

Brum jiggled back and **zigzagged** across the square.

Somebody else was looking at the BIG bunch of balloons too.

Brum revved.

It was a Big Town baddy!

Suddenly the baddy grabbed the balloons and sprinted away.

After him Brum!

Superhero Brum **thundered** through the Big Town.

'You can't catch me,' cried the baddy, as he dashed into the Park and darted behind a tall green hedge.

One by one the balloons peeked over the top. Brum whirled his wheels and raced across the grass.

Follow those balloons Brum!

The balloons wobbled to the left.

And they bobbled to the right.

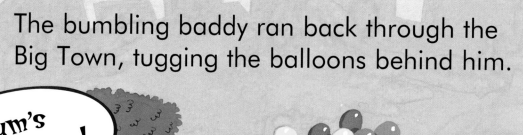

The bumbling baddy ran back through the Big Town, tugging the balloons behind him.

Brum's catching up!

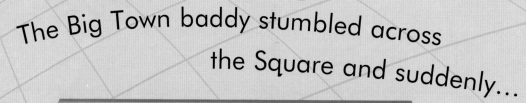

The Big Town baddy stumbled across the Square and suddenly...

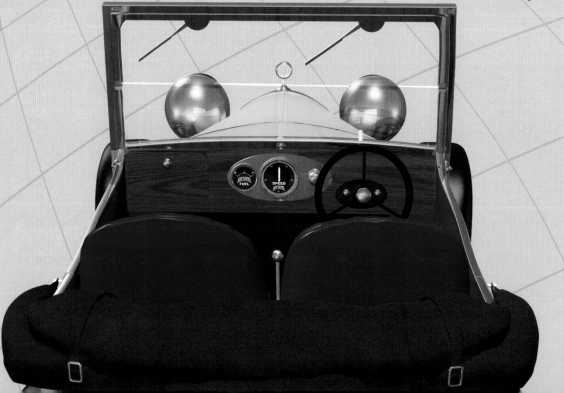

...disappeared!

A bunch of balloons floated slowly out of a hole in the ground.

Brum **hurtled** towards the hole, flapping his doors and wiggling his wings.

Where's the baddy Brum?

The Big Town baddy was down in the hole and stuck in the mud. He wouldn't be getting away.

Brum looked up.

The balloons were floating away! Only their strings were on the ground.

Brum opened his door and scooped up the strings.

Superhero Brum had saved the balloons!

The Big Town balloon seller was very pleased. 'You're the best, Brum,' she said with a smile. Brum jiggled.

Everyone clapped their favourite superstar superhero.

Brum's saved the day!